New Roots Farm Books- Book 1

BEE HELPFUL

Rubee's Happy Hive Series

Written by
Heidi Fowler

Illustrated by
A.C. DeMuth

For my mother, Betty Demuth, who encouraged my imagination, supported my desire to write and read with great anticipation every story and poem I created until the day the angels took her home.

ISBN: 978-1-960858-33-7

Published in the United States of America by:
Cobb Publishing
704 E. Main St.
Charleston, AR 72933
CobbPublishing.com
Editor@CobbPublishing.com

BEE HELPFUL

Rubee took the last bite of the wax capping that covered her cell. For the first time since the egg that she had hatched from was laid (17 days ago), she looked around with her ocelli.

Ocelli (uh-cheh-lee) are a bee's small eyes that help them to see inside of the hive where it is darker. Like all bees, Rubee's ocelli are at the top of her head—all three of them!!

OCELLI

Rubee was awestruck by everything she saw around her. Her home was amazing, and her family was very busy. So busy that they hardly noticed her. They certainly didn't seem to have time to answer her many questions.

"Rubee, there's no time for questions right now. You must eat your pollen and honey, and then you need to clean your cell. There is much to do today!" said Beeatrice, an older sister who was caring for a baby bee that had not hatched yet.

Rubee obediently began cleaning her cell as she instinctively knew she should. She was aware that her cell would be needed by the queen soon. A new egg would be laid in this cell, and twenty days later Rubee would have another sister.

Rubee was almost done cleaning her cell when a bright light suddenly lit up the hive. Rubee looked up through her larger compound eyes and jumped in surprise. Above her was a creature peering in at her and her family!

"Beeatrice!" cried Rubee, "there is a monster in our hive!" The little bee covered all of her eyes in fear.

"Oh Rubee, you silly bee," Beeatrice chuckled. "That is not a monster. That is Annie, our beekeeper."

"Beekeeper?" asked Rubee as she peeked through her front right foreleg. "What is that?"

"A beekeeper is someone who helps us along. They do many different tasks, such as put together our hives, give us more room when our home is full, help us when we are sick and sometimes feed us when pollen is hard to find. Beekeepers care for their bees," Beeatrice explained.

"Don't forget they take our honey!" Another sister bee had moved closer to Rubee and Beeatrice and heard them talking.

"Oh Beeanca!" Beeatrice rolled her compound eyes. "Annie is a good beekeeper. She only takes a little honey, and she always leaves us plenty. She has never left us hungry."

Beeanca thought a minute and then nodded, "I guess you're right, Beeatrice. Annie is a good beekeeper." She finished feeding a baby bee and walked away.

The hive became dark again and Rubee looked up in just enough time to see the top of the hive being put in its place. Annie had taken a peek inside to see how her bees were doing and was now gone, out of sight.

Rubee finished cleaning the last of her cell and a thought struck her. She turned back to Beeatrice, "Is that why Annie takes care of us? So she can have some of our honey?"

Beeatrice smiled, "You ask a lot of questions Rubee." The older bee shook her head and moved to feed the next hungry baby. "Taking some of the honey is one reason Annie keeps bees. But there are other reasons."

Beeatrice cleared her throat and began to explain to her little sister, "Beekeepers know how much bees are needed in this world, Rubee. Bees pollinate the plants that produce the food that people and animals eat. So they want bees to stay healthy and plentiful."

"Beekeepers like Annie have gardens of their own. We use her flowers to gather pollen to bring home for us to use. As we move from flower to flower, a little pollen gets spread to each blossom. That helps the plants produce food!"

Another sister bee joined the conversation, "Don't forget, sometimes beekeepers tend bees in order to help us survive!"

"Yes, Debee, you are right. There are many beekeepers who keep colonies for the sole purpose of keeping bees alive and healthy." Beeatrice nodded at her sister in approval. She pointed at a hungry baby. "Debee, cell number 214 needs some lunch."

The older bee inspected Rubee's cell. "Good job, Rubee! A new sister will soon enjoy this spotless room." Beeatrice turned to face her little sister again, "Still, there are other reasons people take on the job of beekeeping. There's education for example."

"Education? I don't understand," Rubee looked quizzically at Beatrice. She knew she should be helping to clean up around the hive but she had so many questions!

"Yes," said Beeatrice, "beekeepers learn many things by taking care of us. They learn about how valuable we are, how we work, live and communicate. They learn much about nature itself just by caring for us. Then, they take that knowledge and teach others!"

Bobbee, one of Rubee's brothers, was walking by. He stopped to hear Beatrice explain these things.

"Beekeepers also tend bees because they like it," Bobbee interjected. "Beekeeping can be relaxing and fun for some people." The big bee smiled at Rubee and slowly walked away, probably looking for a sister willing to give him a snack.

Beeatrice watched Bobbee for a minute, then turned back to Rubee, "That is true, beekeeping is an interesting and healthy hobby for people."

Rubee thought about all of this new information she learned. Beekeepers definitely didn't sound like monsters; in fact, they sounded a bit interesting to her. She knew that Beeatrice was very busy, but she wanted to add one last comment to the conversation.

"Beekeepers sound like they are very helpful."

"Yes Rubee, they are helpful to us and we are helpful to them. Beeing helpful is important for all of God's creatures. We should always try to help one another. When we do, it makes everyone's life a little easier. Sometimes we all need a hand at getting a job done or help when we are sick. Sometimes we need help because we are hungry and have no food or need shelter because we are homeless. Many times we just need to know that others are there for us."

Beeatrice was finished feeding the baby bees on the frame where Rubee was born. "Well, little sister, I need to move to the next frame and feed the hungry babies there. When you are done cleaning cells here, you can move on as well. It is important that we all keep working together. Remember, bee helpful!"

With that, Beeatrice headed to the next frame in the hive. Rubee turned back to her work and smiled. Another sister was emerging from her cell.

"Hello, little sister!" she said to the newborn bee. "I'm Rubee."

The new bee smiled and looked around in awe, "Hi! I'm Gabbee." She rubbed her abdomen, "I sure am hungry!"

Rubee chuckled, "You need some pollen and honey. And when you are done eating, I'll help you clean your cell."

"Thank you, Rubee!" said the new bee as she gobbled her meal.

"No problem! I'm glad to lend a hand. After all, it's good to bee helpful!"

Let us not lose heart in doing good, for in due time we will reap if we do not grow weary.

Galatians 6:9

Do not merely look out for your own personal interests, but also for the interests of others.

Philippians 2:4

www.ingramcontent.com/pod-product-compliance
Lightning Source LLC
Chambersburg PA
CBHW040900120626
46551CB00001B/107